The
Piñata

Written by Ciaran Murtagh
Illustrated by Eugenia Nobati

Collins

Chapter 1

So far it had been the best birthday ever! I'd opened all my presents and they had been brilliant. I got a remote-controlled car from Mum and Dad, a pencil case from my big brother Carlos, and even my little sister Bonita had given me a present – one of her bright pink scrunchies. Not something I wanted, but she's only five and it's the thought that counts!

After breakfast, my brother, my sister and I sat on the sofa and watched TV while Mum and Dad got things ready for the lunchtime family birthday party. We were going to eat treats, play games and, when we were done, pulverise a piñata with a stick! That was my favourite bit of the party. The piñata is a rainbow-coloured donkey filled with sweets. Every time you hit it, sweets fall from its tummy and you get to eat the ones that you make fall. It is an old family tradition, and everybody looked forward to it.

Because it was my birthday, I got to decide what we watched. I flicked through the channels to see what was on.

Carlos sighed. "Why are you even bothering to look?" he said. "We all know what you're going to choose."

Bonita giggled. "Detective Monkey Brains," she said. "You always choose Detective Monkey Brains!"

They were right. I smiled and flicked the TV to
the right channel. I loved Detective Monkey Brains.
He's a detective monkey who goes around the jungle
solving mysteries. He's cool, clever and funny and when
I grow up, I want to be just like him – apart from the
being a monkey bit!

As the three of us sat and giggled, I thought that the day
couldn't get any better and I was right – it couldn't.
In fact, it was about to get a whole lot worse …

Chapter 2

Mum and Dad had decorated the garden with balloons and streamers, and the piñata hung from the big tree by the pond. As soon as Bonita saw it, she began to sulk.

"It's bigger than the one I had for my birthday," she said.

Dad shook his head. "No," he said. "It's exactly the same and there's the same number of sweets in there too – I counted!"

Mum carried the snacks she'd prepared over
to the garden table.

"I don't know why it has to be filled with sweets,"
she said. "It's so unhealthy."

Dad chuckled. "It's only for special occasions," he said.
"A few sweets on a birthday never hurt anybody."

Everyone laughed. Of course, Dad would say that.
Everybody knew he had a sweet tooth.

As we tucked into the birthday lunch, Mum said
that if we wanted to do the piñata, we needed to
finish lunch first. I bit into an enchilada – they were
Mum's speciality!

Carlos said he couldn't wait for the piñata; he'd been
practising his whacking swing all week. He stood up
and mimed hitting the piñata with a stick.

Everyone laughed and I got a waft of a strange sweet
smell from his direction. Before I could ask him
about it, Mum told him to sit down.

On the other side of the table, Dad was struggling with a napkin. He was trying to shake it off his fingers.

"Silly thing," he said, as it finally came loose. "I've got sticky fingers today!"

We watched him munch on some celery sticks.

"Not the same as piñata sweets," he said, with a wink.

Soon lunch was over, and after we'd helped Mum and Dad tidy away the things, it was time for the piñata. We all lined up by the tree. As it was my birthday, I went first. Dad tied on the blindfold, handed me the special piñata stick and spun me around three times.

"Give it a good whack!" he said, as the rest of the family cheered me on.

I took a deep breath, raised the stick high above my head and swung as hard as I could. The stick connected with the piñata with a loud "thwack"!

"So?" I said, taking off my blindfold. "How many sweets did I get?"

"None," said Bonita. "None at all."

Carlos took the stick from me and pulled on the blindfold.

"You probably didn't hit it hard enough," he said. "Let me try."

He gave the piñata the biggest hit I'd ever seen, but there were still no sweets.

"Impossible!" said Carlos, as he ripped off the blindfold.

"There's something fishy going on here," said Dad, as he reached up and took the piñata off the branch.

He tipped it upside down and gave it a shake. Normally, you could hear the sweets rattling about in there, but this time there was nothing.

"It's empty," said Bonita.

"The sweets have been stolen," said Dad.

Chapter 3

"Who would steal birthday sweets?" gasped Mum.

"Somebody has," said Carlos, "and there's only been us here all day. So, which one of you took the sweets?"

Everyone denied it, and even though I'd had a wonderful birthday, something about the empty piñata left me feeling sad.

"I think I'll just go up to my bedroom for a bit," I said.

As I headed up the stairs, my head was filled with confusion. Who would take the sweets from inside a piñata and why? It was a real mystery.

As I lay on my bed, I looked up at the Detective Monkey Brains poster that hung on the wall and suddenly I knew exactly what to do.

My gran had given me a Detective Monkey Brains detective kit for my birthday – maybe it was time to use it. It had a notebook, a pencil and a cool Detective Monkey Brains voice recorder.

I had a mystery that I needed to solve. Detective Monkey Brains would interview suspects and look for clues. The suspects in this case were my own family, and as I thought about the events of the day, they all seemed like they might have had a reason to take the sweets.

Carlos had been smelling of sweets all day. Was that because he'd taken the sweets and gobbled them up before anyone had had a chance to notice they'd gone? I made a note in the notebook.

1. Interview Carlos.

Then I thought about my little sister. She had been jealous of my piñata, plus she had just the right-sized fingers to sneak her way inside and take the sweets. I made another note.

2. Interview Bonita.

My Dad had a sweet tooth and his fingers had been
sticky at lunchtime. Sticky fingers would be just
the kind of thing you'd have if you'd eaten a load of
sticky birthday sweets. I would be speaking to him too.

3. Interview Dad.

And what about Mum? Surely Mum wouldn't have taken the sweets. But then I remembered what she'd said at the start of the day. She'd said that she thought sweets were unhealthy. Had she taken them because she wanted us to be healthier? Perhaps.

I made one last note in my notebook.

4. Interview Mum.

I looked at my list and smiled to myself. I was going to get to the bottom of the Great Piñata Mystery one way or another, and I was going to start with Carlos.

Chapter 4

Carlos was in his bedroom playing on his console when I found him. He paused the game and flashed me a smile when he saw me come in.

"Bad luck about the piñata, bro," he said. "I wonder where those sweets got to."

I narrowed my eyes and took out my voice recorder.

"I wonder too," I said. "Mind if I ask you a few questions about what you were doing today?"

I clicked on the recorder and asked Carlos some questions.

Me: Did you take the sweets from the piñata?

Carlos: Seriously, bro! As if I'd do something like that. Besides, I'd been practising my swing all week. Why would I do that if I was just going to take them anyway?

Me:　What were you doing this morning?

Carlos:　Well, I gave you your birthday present
　　　and then I set up my camera to record out
　　　of the window.

Me:　Why did you do that?

Carlos:　It's for a school Geography project.
　　　My teacher wants me to sit here for
　　　a whole morning counting birds.
　　　Like I don't have better things to do.
　　　I've recorded everything and then
　　　I'm going to watch it on fast forward
　　　later – clever, huh?

Me:　Last question. Why do you smell
　　　of sweets?

Carlos:　It's my new body spray, bro!
　　　Tutti Frutti – smell it!

He grabbed a can of deodorant from his bedside table and sprayed me with it. I coughed and spluttered. It was the smell I had smelt earlier. It looked like my brother was in the clear.

It was time to speak to my sister.

Chapter 5

Bonita was in her bedroom rearranging her hair clips and scrunchies.

I popped the recorder on the table and asked her my questions.

Me: Did you take my piñata sweets?

Bonita: No. And you're not the only one with things going missing, you know. My scrunchies are missing too. I gave them a wash and put them in the garden to dry, but now they're gone.

Me: I'm not interested in your scrunchies – what about the piñata?

Bonita: I can't even reach it – my legs are too short.

Me: So you didn't take the sweets?

Bonita: No! Anyway, I've got loads of sweets
left from my birthday last month – see?
If I wanted some, I'd just eat those.
So, stop being so silly and help me find
my scrunchies.

Bonita opened a drawer to show me. It was full of
sparkly shiny piñata sweets.

I realised I wasn't going to get anywhere and left Bonita with her accessories. It was clear my brother and sister didn't take the sweets. That meant it had to be Mum or Dad. The net was closing!

Dad was in the shed, tinkering with a lawnmower. I explained what I was doing and asked if he minded being interviewed.

Dad: An interview? Wow! You're watching too much Detective Monkey Brains, buddy! Maybe I need to confiscate that TV remote for a while.

Me: What were you doing this morning?

Dad: What do you think I was doing? Getting ready for your birthday party, of course. I stuffed the piñata with sweets. Then I came upstairs and gave you your present. Then, while Mum got the food ready for the birthday lunch, I hung the piñata up in the tree.

Me: Was it full of sweets?

Dad: Of course it was. No fun having an empty piñata! It was hard to hang though. There was a squirrel who kept on bothering me. I don't think it liked having things hung from its tree – but what can you do? It was only for an hour, wasn't it?

Me: So why did you have sticky fingers?

Dad: Ah! I see what you're getting at.
Sticky fingers from sticky sweets, eh?
Good thinking, but not guilty! I spent
some time gluing your remote-controlled
car together so we can play with it later.
My fingers must have got a bit sticky.

Me: So you didn't take the sweets?

Dad: No way! I'd never take your sweets,
buddy, it wouldn't be right. Besides, don't
tell your mum, but there are always
a few more sweets in the packet than fit
in the piñata. I might have had a couple
before lunch! One of the perks of being
the piñata-packer!

Dad nodded at the model car on the workbench in the corner.

Suddenly I felt bad. He'd been doing something nice for me and I was accusing him of stealing. He threw an arm over my shoulder.

I turned off the recorder. If it hadn't been my brother, my sister or my dad who had taken the sweets – it had to be Mum. I left Dad in the shed and went to find her.

Chapter 6

Mum was in the living room watching her favourite soap. When I came in, she could see that I wanted to talk so she paused the programme.

"Still upset about the piñata?" she asked.

I nodded and explained what I'd been up to.

"Then the only person left to ask is me," said Mum. "Fire away."

I turned on the recorder.

Me: What did you do this morning?

Mum: Well, I was up bright and early wrapping your birthday present. I'd bought a special shiny bow that I was going to stick on, but it went missing.

Me: How?

Mum: I have no idea. I'd popped it on the windowsill while I did the wrapping, but when I went to look for it, it had gone. Maybe your Dad moved it.

Me: Did you see who took the sweets?

Mum: No. I was too busy getting ready for
the lunchtime party.

Me: Did you take the sweets?

Mum: No, why do you think I'd do that?

Me: You said they were unhealthy. Maybe you didn't want us eating them?

Mum: You're right, I do worry about the amount of sugar you eat. But kids should have treats on birthdays. I didn't take your sweets, and I wouldn't lie about it.

I turned off the recorder. In my heart of hearts, I knew she was telling the truth. In my heart of hearts, I didn't think anyone else in my family would take the sweets either. But somebody had, so if not my family, then who?

What was I supposed to do now? I'd spoken to everybody and I was no closer to solving the Great Piñata Mystery.

In my bedroom, I looked at Detective Monkey Brains once again. He always said that the evidence didn't lie, but what were you supposed to do if you didn't have any evidence?

I listened back to my recordings and made some notes in my notebook. As I did, something strange happened. A suspect started to emerge. By the time I'd finished listening, I was sure I knew who had taken the sweets and I even knew how to prove it.

I ran to my brother's bedroom and asked if I could borrow his camera. He nodded and handed it over.

"What's this about?" he asked.

I told him to meet me in the living room and to make sure Mum, Dad and Bonita were there too. I'd explain everything!

Chapter 7

Moments later, my family were all sitting in the living room and I had connected the camera to the TV.

"So," said Dad. "Have you solved the case?"

"I think so," I said. And then I explained what I had discovered.

"My first clue was when Bonita said some of her sparkly scrunchies had disappeared from the garden." I produced the sparkly scrunchie she had given me for my birthday. "But they weren't the only sparkly thing to go missing today. Mum's bow for my present disappeared too."

"I just don't know where it's got to," she said.

"And the other sparkly things to go missing are the piñata sweets," I said. "They're covered in sparkly paper. But who – or what – would take sparkly things from the garden? Then I remembered Dad had told me about a squirrel living in the piñata tree, and I wondered if it might have had something to do with it."

I pressed play on Carlos's camera.

"Thanks to Carlos's Geography project, we might just find out. He filmed the garden all morning. But as well as seeing birds, we might also see a squirrel."

As we watched, we saw Dad put up the piñata and then he went into the shed to make the model car. Once he was gone, we saw the squirrel investigate the piñata and come out with a shiny sweetie. It did it time and time again until the piñata was empty and all the sweeties were in its den.

"The case of the Great Piñata Mystery is solved,"
I said, proudly clicking off the camera.

"And the case of the missing scrunchies," said Bonita.

"And the missing gift bow," said Mum.

Carlos giggled as he ruffled my hair. "Good job, bro!"
he said. "You're just like Detective Monkey Brains.
Only you're not a monkey and you might actually
have brains."

That afternoon, Dad got out a stepladder and peered into the den. He found one sleeping squirrel curled up with three scrunchies, a sparkly bow and lots of sweeties.

After dinner, the whole family assembled in the garden. The piñata had been refilled with sweets and was swinging from the tree.

"Better late than never," I said, and took a swing with the stick. As the sweets rained down from the piñata, the family cheered. This was one family tradition everyone loved, and it wasn't a mystery to see why!

Confession

I admit it. I took the sweets. But how was I supposed to know they weren't for me? I'm just a humble squirrel. As far as I'm concerned, if you hang sweets on my tree and walk away then you're giving me a present! To be honest I didn't even know they were sweets. I thought they were some kind of sparkly nuts. I was hoping they'd see me through hibernation.

I'll give them all back if you want. A few of them might be a bit grubby – my squirrel hole isn't the cleanest place, but you can still eat them. No? Fine! Suit yourself. Maybe I will keep them for hibernation, after all. Now I just need to figure out how to get through the wrapper …

Ideas for reading

Written by Clare Dowdall, PhD
Lecturer and Primary Literacy Consultant

Reading objectives:
- make inferences on the basis of what is being said and done
- answer and ask questions
- predict what might happen on the basis of what has been read so far
- explain and discuss their understanding of books, poems and other material, both those that they listen to and those that they read for themselves

Spoken language objectives:
- give well-structured descriptions and explanations
- speak audibly and fluently with an increasing command of spoken

English
- participate in discussions, presentations, performances and debates

Curriculum links: Design technology; Science – living things and their habitats

Word count: 2933

Interest words: pulverise, tradition, enchilada, suspects, tinkering, confiscate, humble, hibernation

Resources: dictionaries; paper and pencils; ICT for research, materials for making a piñata (balloons, newspaper, paste/glue, paint and decorations)

Build a context for reading

- Ask children about any experiences they have of receiving and breaking open a piñata at a celebration.

- Look at the front cover and read the title. Challenge children to imagine what The Great Piñata Mystery might involve.

- Read the blurb to the children and compare their ideas about the story to the information given. Ask them to predict who has taken the sweets – and why.

Understand and apply reading strategies

- Read pages 2 to 3 as a group. Ask children to describe any birthday traditions that they enjoy (being sensitive to family situations).